Dear Parent:
Your child's love of reading starts here!

Every child learns to read in a different way and at his or her own speed. You can help your young reader improve and become more confident by encouraging his or her own interests and abilities. You can also guide your child's spiritual development by reading stories with biblical values and Bible stories, like I Can Read! books published by Zonderkidz. From books your child reads with you to the first books he or she reads alone, there are I Can Read! books for every stage of reading:

SHARED READING
Basic language, word repetition, and whimsical illustrations, ideal for sharing with your emergent reader.

BEGINNING READING
Short sentences, familiar words, and simple concepts for children eager to read on their own.

READING WITH HELP
Engaging stories, longer sentences, and language play for developing readers.

READING ALONE
Complex plots, challenging vocabulary, and high-interest topics for the independent reader.

ADVANCED READING
Short paragraphs, chapters, and exciting themes for the perfect bridge to chapter books.

I Can Read! books have introduced children to the joy of reading since 1957. Featuring award-winning authors and illustrators and a fabulous cast of beloved characters, I Can Read! books set the standard for beginning readers.

A lifetime of discovery begins with the magical words **"I Can Read!"**

Visit www.icanread.com for information on enriching your child's reading experience.
Visit www.zonderkidz.com for more Zonderkidz I Can Read! titles.

A friend loves at all times. He is
there to help when trouble comes.
—*Proverbs 17:17*

Otter and Owl and the Big Ah-choo!
Copyright © 2008 by Crystal Bowman
Illustrations copyright © 2008 by Kevin Zimmer

Requests for information should be addressed to:
Zonderkidz, Grand Rapids, Michigan 49530

Library of Congress Cataloging-in-Publication Data:

Bowman, Crystal.
  Otter and Owl and the big ah-choo! / written by Crystal Bowman; illustrated by Kevin Zimmer.
     p. cm. – (I can read. Level 1)
  ISBN 978-0-310-71705-8 (softcover : alk. paper) [1. Friendship-Fiction. 2. Sneezing-Fiction. 3. Christian life-Fiction.] I. Zimmer, Kevin, ill. II. Title.
  PZ7.B6834Ot 2008
  [E]--dc22
                                                                                                          2008009581

Art Direction and Design: Jody Langley

Printed in China

08 09 10 • 4 3 2 1

I Can Read!

Otter and Owl and the Big Ah-choo!

story by Crystal Bowman

pictures by Kevin Zimmer

Owl sat on a stump by the pond.

He was wearing a new green cap.

His friend Otter came by.

"I like your green cap," said Otter.

"Thanks," said Owl. "I like it too."

"What shall we do today?" asked Otter.

"Let me think about it," said Owl.

Then Otter started to sneeze.

Ah-choo! Ah-choo! Ah-choo!

"Bless you," said Owl.

Ah-choo! Otter sneezed again.

He blew the cap off Owl's head.

"Whoops! I'm sorry

I blew off your cap," said Otter.

Otter looked at the yellow flowers.

"I think flowers make me sneeze,"
said Otter.

Owl put the cap back on his head.

"Let's go to my house," Owl said.

"I don't have flowers in my house."

Otter and Owl went to Owl's house.

Owl got out his train set.

"Let's make a train track," he said.

"And we can make a tunnel too."

Owl made a track for the train.

Otter made a tunnel for the train.

Ah-choo! Ah-choo! Ah-choo!

Otter sneezed.

"Bless you," said Owl.

Ah-choo! Otter sneezed again.

He blew the cap off Owl's head.

"I'm sorry," said Otter.

"I think trains make me sneeze."

Owl shook his head.

Then he put on his cap.

"Let's go to your house," he said.

Otter and Owl went to Otter's house.

"Let's watch cartoons," said Owl.

Otter and Owl sat on the big sofa

to watch the cartoons.

Ah-choo! Ah-choo! Ah-choo!

Otter began to sneeze again.

"What's making you sneeze now?" asked Owl.

"Maybe it's the TV," said Otter.

"Let me think about it," said Owl.

Owl thought and thought and thought.

Then Owl got a sad look on his face.

"I know the problem," said Owl.

"Your TV doesn't make you sneeze.

My train doesn't make you sneeze.

And flowers don't make you sneeze."

"What is it then?" asked Otter.

"It's me!" cried Owl.

"I make you sneeze!"

"Oh no!" cried Otter.

"This is awful!"

Ah-choo! Otter sneezed again.

He blew the cap off Owl's head.

"We can't be friends," said Owl.

He put his cap back on his head.

"Good-bye, Otter," said Owl.

"Good-bye, Owl," said Otter.

Owl walked to his house.

Then he turned around
and went back to Otter's house.

"Here," said Owl.

"I want you to have my green cap."

"I can't take it," said Otter.

"You like your new green cap."

"I want you to wear it," said Owl.

"It will make you think about me."

"Okay," said Otter. "I will wear it.

And I will think about you.

But I will miss you."

"I will miss you too," said Owl.

Owl went to his house.

He did not play with his train.

He did not watch cartoons.

He just thought about Otter.

Then he prayed, "Dear God,
please take care of Otter.
He was a good friend."

Knock! Knock! Knock!

Owl heard someone at his door.

It was Otter.

"Go away," said Owl.

"I make you sneeze."

Otter laughed and laughed.

"You don't make me sneeze.

Your new green cap makes me sneeze!"

"Really?" asked Owl.

"Yes, really!" said Otter.

Owl put his green cap in his closet
and shut the door tight.

Otter and Owl
watched cartoons.

Then they played
with the train set.

They even played
out by the flowers.

They were glad to be friends again.

Otter did not sneeze anymore.